## About the Author

Brendan Sloane lives on planet earth with all the other human beings and creatures. One day he will be recycled back into the mother earth that he came from. But until then he lives with his beautiful wife and son in Canberra, Australia. After commuting recently for eight years in London, he felt a desire to create a guide for people, so they know what they are getting themselves into when entering the London Underground.

# A BODACIOUS GUIDE TO THE LONDON UNDERGROUND

**Brendan Sloane**

# A BODACIOUS GUIDE TO THE LONDON UNDERGROUND

Vanguard Press

A CIP catalogue record for this title is
available from the British Library.

ISBN 978 1 78465 612 6

*Vanguard Press is an imprint of
Pegasus Elliot MacKenzie Publishers Ltd.
www.pegasuspublishers.com*

First Published in 2020

**Vanguard Press
Sheraton House Castle Park
Cambridge England**

Printed & Bound in Great Britain

# Dedication

This book is dedicated to all the people who 'walk the line' in the London Underground.

## Disclaimer

No advice in the book should be taken seriously or followed. In fact, be nice to people on the London Underground. Be like Jesus or someone else who is reportedly really nice. The London Underground only works due to the collective politeness of all involved.

# In the Beginning

The London Underground has been around for over seven million years. This is a fact! Nobody really knows who built it or how it works. Some say a giant humanoid race of rats built it. Scholars and historians maintain it was the results of a rare high-speed collision of a flux capacitor and a black hole near our sun at the same time a temporal warp opened up subcutaneous to our planet – this caused a rift that sent blasts of energy through wormholes in our space-time continuum. Plausible as the train filled catacombs of the London Underground do look like large wormholes!

It is important to understand that given it was never created by humans, it was never really intended for us, which is why there is so much dysfunctional human behaviour occurring within its confines. Using this enigmatic rail system is literally running a hazardous social and physical gauntlet daily. I stand mere inches from a violent end every morning on my way to work. One push or even the quick movement of body organs due to say, a sneeze could be enough to push my existence the extra three inches forward that would see my vessel of life shredded into pasta-like strips – it would come with sauce too, let me tell you!

The social behaviour or carnage I refer to is the number of gaffs, lapses and bloomers the average person makes that can lead to a major disruption in life. Sometimes a five-minute delay due to some numpty dumpty who looks like they are barely aware of gravity let alone the multifaceted London Underground, can lead to a divorce or loss of a job! Perhaps that late five minutes will be considered the 'last time you will ever be late' by some inimical employer or zealous and unforgiving partner. Can you imagine!

Of course, I have drawn this example from real life. I knew a man who was five minutes late to a meeting, and he did lose his job, then his wife left him, and he contracted a rare flesh-eating bug! Yep, he did and all because he and several hundred other commuters were stuck behind some village idiot bouncing off the walls like a pinball within the tunnel connecting Kings Cross and St Pancreas. It can be hard to imagine a person acting like a pinball in a tunnel without actually hurting themselves enough that would ensure they rid themselves and others of their inconvenience. But, if an individual acquires several bad behavioural traits, they can be seen sort of 'skeleton dancing' down a passage or tunnel, never really hurting themselves but causing more chaos than a loose tennis ball in a dog pound. I've not seen old mate for a while and rumour has it he wanders the Underground in bedraggled pyjamas, only ever stopping for the occasional sip of water and a bacon sarnie... and all because of a five-minute delay. True story.

So, if you want to avoid these sorts of life-compounding cataclysms and not end up looking like the village idiot within the Underground's rotund belly, I suggest you take heed. Read on and let me shine a light down a very dark and uncomfortable sweaty tunnel... Let me introduce you to a few of the daily vagabonds that you will need to avoid like the plague. Then, maybe, just maybe you will survive...

# 1. The Snail

Let's start with the biggest purveyor of chaos, the snail or the slowpoke. I once witnessed a person walking so slowly, it looked like they were going backwards at an accelerating pace. Kind of like an optical illusion – the legs WERE moving forward AND in the correct kinesiological manner but somehow… somehow they were sliding backwards like some badly pixelated video game character from the '80s edging or moonwalking to the left of your screen because your computer overheated. I witnessed this, and sometimes you must just walk away lest you be caught up in it. It was reported on the news later that night and, rumour has it, they set out to work on a Tuesday and ended up arriving the previous Monday morning!

This is an extreme example of course. I have watched people and often thought I wonder if they have to pack up and head home after arriving at work? – as it could take several hours for them to get to their work destination, given the lack of forward momentum in their leg strides. Perhaps they spend their entire life walking to and from work, only able to give ten to twenty minutes of productive work per day.

Slow walking can catch on too, like a disease. I once witnessed a gaggle of snails moving through a very narrow tunnel which caused people to stack up behind them, creating a wall of humans. They stacked up to the roof looking like some macabre human rainbow crush – kind of a cross between the human centipede and one of Genghis Khan's pile of heads. I heard later they just filled in that tunnel with concrete as it was too late for all involved. Collateral damage, I guess.

**Approach:** Just push past them – a quick kick to the heel from behind will usually be enough for them to slow down to a whole new supersonic slow and you will be able to pass these people even if you stand still. You won't have to worry about them chasing you consequently, given that their legs clearly don't work properly.

## 2. The Backpack Shack Attack

I am not going to mince my words here. A backpack does not belong on the Underground, EVER. Therefore, a satchel, or a man bag was invented so that people were not carrying something the magnitude of a small shed behind them. Usually, these people are oblivious to the wreckage of humanity they leave in their wake. They don't have to witness the carnage as they are always facing away from it. They are like a wakeboard or a jet ski through a crowd, as people fall in behind then get thrown to the left and right like dust particles. As the backpack fuckwit turns a corner, their body turns, which of course means the protruding port-a-loo attached to their back shifts at a speed faster than a whip cracking and is sent into an oncoming pedestrian. This will usually result in multiple smashed bones and pulverised marrow. Annoyingly, the backpack shack will be whistling Dixie twenty metres away, oblivious to the fact someone is receiving CPR behind them because their chest just took a torpedo hit, resulting in what now looks like a roast pig at a medieval banquet –

ribs and flesh reaching for the sky.

It takes a lot to pulverise bone marrow let me tell you! So, you can imagine the knock-on or domino effect of dozens of people falling over. I was once somewhere in the elongated depths of Waterloo station when I heard a low rumble. As I looked up, I saw 'people-dominos' rounding a corner and coming towards me. The air was punctuated with screams of panic and soft thuds as people were felled like trees. I was wearing a helmet that day, so I was OK in the end. I heard afterwards the domino effect had started at Moor Park station and worked its way through to Waterloo. Have a look at a tube map, and you will realise this is close to fucking impossible. But some wannabe Bear Grylls anthropoid was wearing a backpack that looked like a marginally smaller version of the Guggenheim.

**Approach:** Not only have I given away the fact that I wear a helmet in the Underground, but I also always carry scissors with me. Really big ones that can cut through the strap of a backpack even if it is made from car seat straps. You know what to do but, beware, do not get caught in the slipstream as these people turn a corner, otherwise you will be pulverised like stepped-on chalk. On a side note, I also wear knee pads and shin pads. My helmet is a motor cross helmet with full visor and visual digital readouts. Heat detectors, too, which help spot the crowded areas before you reach them. With twenty-four-inch scissors strapped to my thigh, I do resemble something from Mad Max… but then like Max and his mad posse, I am a survivor… read on.

# 3. The Double Handler

A frustrating character who can add a big ol' wodge of anxiety to your day. Often mistaken for two criss-crossed ski poles wedged into an unmoveable ice glacier, they seem unable or unsatisfied to hold a train pole with one hand. They need to spread their legs for stability and stretch to the sky with both hands until they find two firm hand grips. You never want to be near these people as they nearly always hold this position for the entirety of the trip like they are now part of the architecture.

Despite the underarm stench you will be subjected to, these meat bags often take up the space of several people and can then cause a severe 'human crunch' section where the several people who should be standing comfortably in the area that the double handler has taken, are now pressed together like several stamped-on, melted chocolate bars. You will often not be able to tell where one person ends and the next person begins, such is the crush.

**Approach:** Easily the most vulnerable of the Underground train cretins, given their soft fleshy midsections are exposed. One quick aggressive karate chop to the ribs will see this bridge-like person collapse faster than Venice's Rialto Bridge with too many wedding guests.

Nothing more to add here, other than this sentence I have just added. Imperative, I think you will agree!

# 4. The Statue of David

An irksome but rare man-character who is often hard to spot unless you are pushed up against them in some hard to breathe mosh-pit like scenario – by then it is too late of course. You will notice how unyielding and rigid they are. These are a man's man... Y'know? The type who consider pushing a bayonet through someone's belly and out their eye a rite of passage to becoming a 'real' man. This drill sergeant will tense their body so that they command every inch of their 'battle lines' and no matter how hard you push against them they will NEVER move an inch as this would represent an attenuation of their masculinity. This character will often be overheard stating that 'what the snowflake generation needs is a good war'.

You must also watch them walking as they resemble a big baby with a nappy on, legs spread apart when they walk as if they have an arsenal in their pants and require ventilation to protect them from friction burn.

**Approach:** Easily the most volatile and potentially violent of the Underground troglodytes.

Avoid at all costs if you can. Unfortunately, you will have to endure your journey feeling like you are pushed up against a fortification constructed from cubic boron nitrate. There is no approach, and there is no hope.

The real danger is being caught in between two statues of David. Remember the garbage crusher in Star Wars when Luke and Chewie and the whole posse were rescuing some ungrateful princess? Imagine if that R2-D2 unit was not there to stop the impending mash. If this happens to you, you will come out looking like space garbage, legs and arms bent in an impossible direction. You may emerge with a face looking like a melted gumboot, dropped pie, smashed crab or a dead end. The original structure of your face will determine the gruesome outcome, which is why I included four examples. Let's go again! You may emerge with a face looking like a burnt rope, a ballerina's toes, a wet bag of grubs or an earthquake.

# 5. The Tourist AKA the Star Gazer

Let's get something straight. After several years of commuting daily and to dozens of different destinations within the jumbled labyrinth, I can tell you with absolute confidence that there is no reason EVER to look up. There are no trains coming from above you, and there is no map on the roof or even any advertising.

Tourists or star gazers as I like to call them seem to walk around at quarter pace staring at the roof like they are following a UFO around. I don't mind the fact they stare upwards like a minion looking for some escape from the inevitable horizontal fate of entering a big steel worm. Perhaps they have tube commitment phobia? Where if you enter a train there is no going back, and you could end up somewhere in an English 'border town' like Whitby. Can you imagine!

**Approach:** These nomadic wanderers are pack animals and slow like a herd of cows. Like cows though, they can panic, scatter and trample if they are spooked. Once that happens, you may as well abandon the commute and head home. I cannot offer any more advice other than this: like walking a tightrope you need to find the balance between stealth and calmness, lest they get startled and scatter like hippos protecting their young. Once the herd shifts its direction you could find yourself sprawled over two metallic tracks looking into two headlights bearing down on your sorry ass. Game over.

# 6. The Pole Hugger

True to their namesake these people hug poles like I would imagine a pirate hugs the mast of their ship in the middle of a storm except it is more of a squall in the Underground. The trains follow a linear pathway; they are not rattling around like they are poised on the edge of a Hungry Hippos board game. So, there is really no need to straddle the pole like some desperate teenager looking for a sexy chum but settling for anything horizontal.

The worst thing is, several people can hold onto that pole but not when some freak-show is bestriding it. Now those several people must reach elsewhere to maintain balance as they hurtle through the polygonal rat's nest. Seven people, so that's more than thirteen arms that need to find confident latching. The area becomes an eruption of arms that, if all moved at once, could result in systemic human assault, both sexual and physical. If you got caught up in this spider web of a cluster fuck, you could imagine uttering the words 'I'm so sorry my armpit is pressed up against your crotch and the back of my knee up against your face'. In any situation other than the London Underground you would be facing jail time.

**Approach:** Slowly and carefully push your fingers around the pole near their lower stomach – the stomach area is important as it will be an affront to their personage but not enough to be considered assault. A strange smile will also help avoid being a criminal act – think of Jim Carrey for 'strange smile' inspiration. Unlike the statue of David, the pole-hugger will relinquish their stance. The combination of this smile and your fingers slowly rubbing against their soft fleshy tum-tum will be enough to make them jump like an Olympian. You can use the pole now like a normal person.

# 7. The Side-Swiper

Now here is a real oddity of a person. So, a train pulls up, you can feel the slight push from behind which is borne from the collective thrill or anticipation of the 387 people behind you, that they are about to crawl into the shiny steel worm built for twenty-three people. The doors open, the passengers depart, and YOU are the first person on. What do you do? Do you file in and head to the far end of the carriage, thus allowing room for others to follow...? OR like some fucking Xenomorph cocooned to the wall do you stop at the very entrance because you like to hold onto the handrail, thus blocking half the entrance for the 386 other people? Make no mistake, these cretins are the worst – newsflash, you lollipops, you've just halved the entry point of said steel slug. The results? Well you don't want to have chosen the side that this narcissist has decided is entirely theirs because you won't get on. You'll lose your job, your wife, and you may even die a horrible and slow death (who can say) and all because you were five minutes late. Because cocoon pants likes his 'liddle rail' spot many lives may be irrevocably and potentially damaged.

**Approach:** It took me a long time to figure out the approach to this lot. Rage can block clear synapse pathways in your brain, so all I could think of was taking to these secretions with a flamethrower, like Drake in Aliens. Calmness is required because you WILL get angry at them as they look at you sheepishly with puppy dog eyes that say, 'sorry there was nothing I could do'.

So, take a deep breath, close your eyes and simply, slowly but methodically walk into them. It will feel strange but imagine how freaked it makes them. I've tried it after years of frustration, and it works. True Story. It catches them totally unaware as they expect everyone to politely walk around them. They are counting on your politeness – extend to them none and bring an end to their apathetic tyranny with the slow 'walk through'.

# 8. Underground Zombies

Unfortunately, the mobile phone zombies represent about 99% of the current traffic within the train bowels of London. On a slow march to fucking nowhere, you can easily come across several thousand of these bright light worshipping monkeys. With their necks in a constant bend downwards like a broken ladder, I am surprised they do not all walk in front of oncoming trains like lemmings, creating some blood and guts soup that makes each tunnel look like slow-moving lava cascading from one end to the other... wherever the hell THAT may be. (Nobody knows where the Underground starts or finishes.) In 1472, a Royal Commission was appointed to determine the boundaries. It was quickly determined that the Underground is similar to the Universe, forever expanding and therefore impossible to define – a rail tundra that swells and sprouts in a sporadic and capricious nature. Dozens of intrepid explorers and scientists have been sent into its murky depths never to return to the land of the living again. You will never be able to ringfence this beast into a coherent mass or a definable measurement. After all, the corners have straight bits and the straight bits have corners! Figure that one out Pythagoras.

**Approach:** If someone is on their phone, then they have made their choice in life. Choose reality dude, not the digital brain drainer. I guess what I am saying is that I don't consider them to be there as they are in the digital 'multiverse', so if someone is not there, just push them onto the tracks. Many may consider this murder, but as I said, they were never there in the first place... your honour.

Perhaps this is the way to send these digital lemmings into the depths of no return. We would only be culling the 'sheeple' anyway, so it could be viewed as a Darwinian chlorination of the gene pool. Nobody who looks at their phone for more than a few hours a day is ever going to contribute to the human race (actually many do).

# 9. The Village Idiot

Usually, UK residents on 'their big trip to London town' have come from places with a population akin to a single London street. Easily the loudest on the Underground as, like many English holidaymakers, they arrive drunk and continue to be drunk until the very last minute they leave the urban human and concrete farm that is London. These drifters and serfs are probably the most harmless and to be honest I quite like 'em. Why? Because they entertain and I am partial for a bit of banter with a stranger – I like to test my social skills in elevators as it is very challenging to make someone feel comfortable to talk in an elevator and even harder to make them laugh. Go on, give it a go. You'll fail miserably initially, but you will only get better.

The village idiot never knows where they are so they will constantly make premature and quick movements for the exit, then realise it is not the right exit to get off so then dart back to their original position like some Mexican fighting fish circling their enclosure. If only we had a small fishbowl to contain them though as they can be dizzying to watch.

**Approach:** Easy, don't make eye contact and you will never have to deal with a village idiot. Make contact though and you will hear all about their village, their borough, their parents and sometimes intimate health details – like the time they got gangrene on their anus because they sat down on a grove of mushrooms… in their bathroom.

# 10. The Gap Buffer

Sometimes the train you are on can become more packed than a Californian hip-hop artist's bong, but you must get on as you may have let three trains go by in your quest to find one that is slightly less heaving. So, there you are, feeling like a lizard pressed between a steel boot and a tennis racquet while some chap has stopped prematurely halfway down the aisle so that they have a gap in front of them, allowing them to check their dumb phone. While your lungs are being crushed, this person has enough room to do a pirouette and is always oblivious to the packed meat tray behind them. They will often have headphones on, a complete lack of peripheral vision and even slightly sway to their music as they are fresh, comfortable and without care.

Meanwhile, your feet are no longer touching the ground, and you are not sure if the ground is the roof or the roof is the ground, as the hurtling carriage is making the meat box group of humans near you slowly slink and shift around like a Jenga in a bucket of jelly. You will not end this trip where you started.

**Approach:** Not much you can do here if you are too far away, other than shout at them to move down, which can often make you look like the aggressor. If you are next to them, it is up to you to free the people behind you by just nudging them slightly. They are harmless, just oblivious, so there is no outrageous approach here, sorry. That said, you can always try licking their ear from behind if you want them to scuttle off.

# 11. The Un-cleansed

No real mystery here. Sometimes an event happens in someone's life where they have consequently decided that cleaning their bodies with a combination of water and soap on a regular basis (more than once a month) is no longer required. Who can say why? Perhaps they lost their job and wife and contracted some horrible disease because of some slow numpty dumpty in the Underground, and decided showers were no longer required.

Either way, there you are, pressed up against a turgid soul who smells like something between a wet dog and a salty cheddar cheese tsunami. How do you get out of this situation because as we know, it will take a week to rid yourself of the stench. You may lose your job, or your wife! And probably stop showering.

**Approach:** The sensible approach is to get off the carriage at the next stop and move into the next one. The fun approach is to start gagging on the train and making spluttering noises like you are finding it hard to breathe – do this near the offender and look at them the entire time. Never underestimate the power of embarrassment as it can be a fantastic conduit for change. You could be helping this person by shaming them into cleaning themselves more often, which may result in a new job or promotion or even a new partner.

# 12. The Panic Exiter

A wallflower librarian type character that you will not notice until you are nearing a station. These people are premature-exiters that cause more fucking chaos than a headless chicken in a snake pit. In other words, they prepare themselves for exiting the train and explode into a flurry of movement well before it is time to exit the train and they do it with such a level of panic, anyone would think their firstborns were at risk of the slave trade in some Taken type scenario. These people are not exemplary of a specific set of skills though, quite the opposite. Such is their level of fear of not being able to get off the train when the doors open, they lose all sense of social awareness, and with eyes dilating and diverting in quick succession they barge through whoever is in between them and the door like a bowling ball.

**Approach:** Remember these people are usually the reserved type so you may never see them coming, but they will come at you like a bat out of hell. Leadership is required. A good hard slap in the face will bring them out of their internal panic room where you will be able to explain to them 'I am getting off too, so there is no need to push past me like it's the Californian land rush and you're trying to jam your stake into the ground before the cowboy beside you does'. Smile the whole time as you have just assaulted them, but the smile will momentarily confuse them into staring blankly at you. Turn around, block them and wait. Don't worry, the most a librarian will ever do is throw a book at you. Just don't let them photograph you or you might find a different book thrown at you. (See what I did there!)

# 13. The Pinball or the Dancing Skeleton

A spectacular combination of several traits within this book, crammed into one bag of meat and bones, these people are a walking cluster fuck of chaotic proportions you will hope never to witness.

They resemble a cross between a meth addict and a bungee cord. Did you ever own a rubber skeleton with a cord attached to it when you were a kid? That is the best way to picture them as they look half suspended in air and seem utterly out of control of their limbs like a puppet master is jiggling them around from above. These people are a mystery to science. As we know though, science is as reliable as a starving monkey. On a side note, it may seem like a lazy metaphor there but get back to me if you ever see a starving monkey in action. There is a good chance you will be getting back to me without your face so it will be difficult to tell me about it.

I have a theory so, who knows, maybe this theory will be considered 'science' one day, until it changes of course. My theory is that due to several disorders or syndromes mentioned in this book, a person can go completely mad and end up tittering and jittering down the hallways, half dead. For example, imagine you start your journey. You enter a train, narrowly avoiding the carnage of a side-swiper who has caused a jumble of humans to fall into 'the gap' only to walk straight into the path of a group of pole huggers and a gaggle of village idiots. The combination of which causes hysteria due to some panic-exiter bowling you all down. You stand dazed and confused by the fact you started in carriage 3 but are now in carriage 11. In your dazed and confused state, you bring yourself to your feet to notice that you are now being slowly crushed in between two statues of David. By this time, you have forgotten your name and the reason why you got on the train in the first place. Suddenly, lying on the ground seems like the next best life-decision. You scramble off at Victoria station only to look up and see approximately 100,000-star gazers heading your way, and you drop to your knees. It's over. After a short nap you find yourself skeleton dancing through the Underground never to regain consciousness again. You are the pinball wizard, my friend.

**Approach:** Run.

# In the End...

I wanted to share some of the experiences on the London Underground that inspired this book as you really do see some strange and exotic human behaviour. I imagine this is because some people who use the Underground would not be caught up in this 'elevator-style' social situation in other cities of the world that don't have trains. An individual may have driven to work in a car their entire life but then find themselves sharing the same 'car' to work with all manner of humans. So, you find yourself crammed up against people in a sweaty and strange situation. It is not natural, but always remember, no matter what happens you will never see any of the individuals again on your commute as they number in the millions.

So, if you do poop your pants due to a stomach bug that hits your lower intestine like an anvil in a Road Runner cartoon at eight thirty a.m., just close your eyes and get through it, because no one will ever recognise you again as the Hunchback of Notre Dame ambling through a train with a mud farm sliding down your leg. Here are some of the best I have witnessed...

# Story 1 – The Person Punt

Within a packed crowd in Stratford, I witnessed a man kick a woman in the bot-bot, and she popped into the air like a football. Before I go any further, I must mention that Stratford station is like the Amazon river – there are more beginnings, endings and merges than the strings on a tennis racquet. You can find yourself happily walking along in a strong mob of commuters and then suddenly be hit from the left by an oncoming flood of busy angry humans. Their direction is different to yours, so it really is like two rivers meeting, but the contents of these rivers are not water particles, rather people, so strange things can happen. Anyway, this tiny lady had a real power walk happening and was swinging her arms as she strode, with real venom. I say venom as she struck a man with her elbow in the groin who doubled over like… well, a man struck in the groin can only double over. She was oblivious, and he was angry at such oblivion, so he chased after her and kicked her like a football. She flew a few metres, landed and kept going with a quick 'fuck you' over the shoulder. Nobody blinked an eye.

# Story 2 – The Inimical Boss

I had a boss who was somewhat of a dickhead. I know what you are thinking; perhaps I am the dickhead. After all, it is all perspective, right? Let me explain – he liked to hold meetings that started at seven thirty a.m. and if you were five minutes late, the meeting was cancelled. That's how busy he was you see. Probably busier than you and me and all our Facebook friends put together.

Anyway, I knew this fact in my first week of work as others in the office had warned me, so I made sure I left an extra thirty minutes for my commute. As luck would have it, we pulled up to Kings Cross station and a fucking window falls out of the train carriage I was in. Just pops out like a Pringle, like it was always meant to pop out at that exact time and morning I had a meeting with Mr Seven-Thirty-a.m.-Crazy-Pants. Anyway, I was impressed with the appearance of workmen, like a SWAT team dropping from the roof, who just appeared there seconds after the incident with all sorts of ratchety, winchety equipment. They worked on replacing that window silently like telepathic ants, but that was not enough to save me from entering the dragon's lair at exactly 7.37 a.m. He then spent twenty minutes lecturing me on professionalism like a nun from the 8th century, all guilt and vitriol. I did not lose my job, but I think I came close to it. You see, a five-minute delay (OK seven minutes) can lead to detrimental consequences to your life. You need to get out of people's way when they get that wild-eyed look in their face, and they are flying down a tunnel like a Ferrari with three wheels, which leads me into my next story…

# Story 3 – Man on a Mission

This guy inspired the dancing skeleton as, if he was not in a life or death situation, then he was on meth or speed or both. Perhaps he had just murdered someone, as he was running down a train platform like a lunatic escaped from the asylum... or perhaps he was working for Mr Seven-Thirty-a.m.-Crazy-Fucking-Pants. His eyes were rolling around in his head like marbles in steel pipes, and he was moving. I mean, if you did not get out of his way, then he was going through you like the Hulk would go through a brick wall. There was no mercy or safety net to his chosen style of movement. He was like a stealth bomber among tractors.

The doors of the train carriages are closing, and I am watching, thinking he cannot make this, unfortunately, he is a metre or two from success – lazy bastard should have moved faster! He obviously realises this, makes a quick Pythagoras inspired mathematical computation and launches himself into the air like a javelin, tucking arms down his side for maximum aerodynamics. He lands with a colossal thud with his head just over the line and inside the train. The train doors crack into his head, retract, and he gets up, dusts himself off and holds onto the pole like it was just another Tuesday. Bravo I thought and gave a little golfers clap... Perhaps he DID make the meeting at seven thirty a.m.

# Story 4 – The Intolerant One

This guy inspired the Backpack Shack Attack as he used his backpack as a weapon on me. His impatient actions sent me hurtling through the air with a quick vehement twist of the shoulder. Let me rewind a little. You see, I was the last person on the train and wedged in the middle of the entrance up against the sliding doors. When we came up to the next stop, almost every person on the train wanted to get off, and the platform we stopped at was jam-packed with nowhere for me to step off thus allowing commuters to get past me. So, I had to impersonate one of the Mario brothers in a Nintendo platform game, ducking and weaving, sliding and jiving and bobbing and tucking. Only problem was, there were too many humans and no mushroom to boost me. Then, suddenly, two people were coming at me from the left and one from the right all at the same time. So, I moved to the right to let the two people coming from the left off the train – block one momentarily to let two off, right? This meant that the guy I was blocking for perhaps two seconds was not happy

– about as happy as a gremlin in a microwave. He shifted slightly so that his backpack wedged up against me and then as I was uttering the words to him, 'Sorry, I am just letting these two people off the—' he unleashes a body twist so sadistic and pugnacious the backpack lifts me into the air and sends me hurtling off the train like a shuttlecock. He only had another second to wait! Unfortunately for him, I was netted by several commuters on the platform and like a trampoline, they catapulted me backwards towards The Intolerant One. So, I am pressed up against my antagonist and in what can only be described as default Australian social behaviour, I spat, 'Are you fucking serious?' and pushed him back. He muttered something about a seven thirty a.m. meeting, and we both went our separate ways.

Lightning Source UK Ltd.
Milton Keynes UK
UKHW051700050323
417907UK00015B/83